I Was Only Nineteen

For
Denny Schumann (nee Storen)
Mick Storen
Frank Hunt
~John Schumann

The illustrator would like to acknowledge in particular the books of Peter Haran.
The vivid descriptions, and detail, in these firsthand stories was invaluable.

First published in 2014

Allen & Unwin
83 Alexander Street
Crows Nest NSW 2065
Australia
Phone: (61 2) 8425 0100
Email: info@allenandunwin.com
Web: www.allenandunwin.com

A Cataloguing-in-Publication entry is available from
the National Library of Australia
www.trove.nla.gov.au

ISBN 978 1 74331 723 5

Teachers' notes available from www.allenandunwin.com

Cover and text design by Sandra Nobes
Set in 20 pt Bauer Bodoni by Sandra Nobes
Colour reproduction by Splitting Image, Clayton, Victoria
This book was printed in April 2014 at Hang Tai Printing (Guang Dong) Ltd.,
Xin Cheng Ind Est. Xie Gang Town, Dong Guan, Guang Dong Province, China.

3 5 7 9 10 8 6 4

The song 'I Was Only 19' is available through iTunes:
https://itunes.apple.com/au/album/i-was-only-19-single/id632696107
More about John, and the song: www.schumann.com.au/john

I Was Only Nineteen

Words by John Schumann
Pictures by Craig Smith

ALLEN&UNWIN
SYDNEY · MELBOURNE · AUCKLAND · LONDON

Mum and Dad and Denny saw the
passing-out parade at Puckapunyal.
(It was a long march from cadets.)

The Sixth Battalion was the next to tour and it was me who drew the card. We did Canungra and Shoalwater before we left.

And Townsville lined the footpath as we marched down to the quay.
This clipping from the paper shows us young and strong and clean.
And there's me in my slouch hat, with my SLR and greens.

God help me, I was only nineteen.

From Vung Tau, riding Chinooks, to the dust at Nui Dat,
I'd been in and out of choppers now for months.
But we made our tents a home, VB and pin-ups on the lockers,
and an Asian orange sunset through the scrub.

And can you tell me, doctor, why I still can't get to sleep?
And night-time's just a jungle dark and a barking M16?
And what's this rash that comes and goes – can you tell me what it means?

God help me, I was only nineteen.

A four-week operation, when each step
could mean your last one on two legs:
it was a war within yourself.

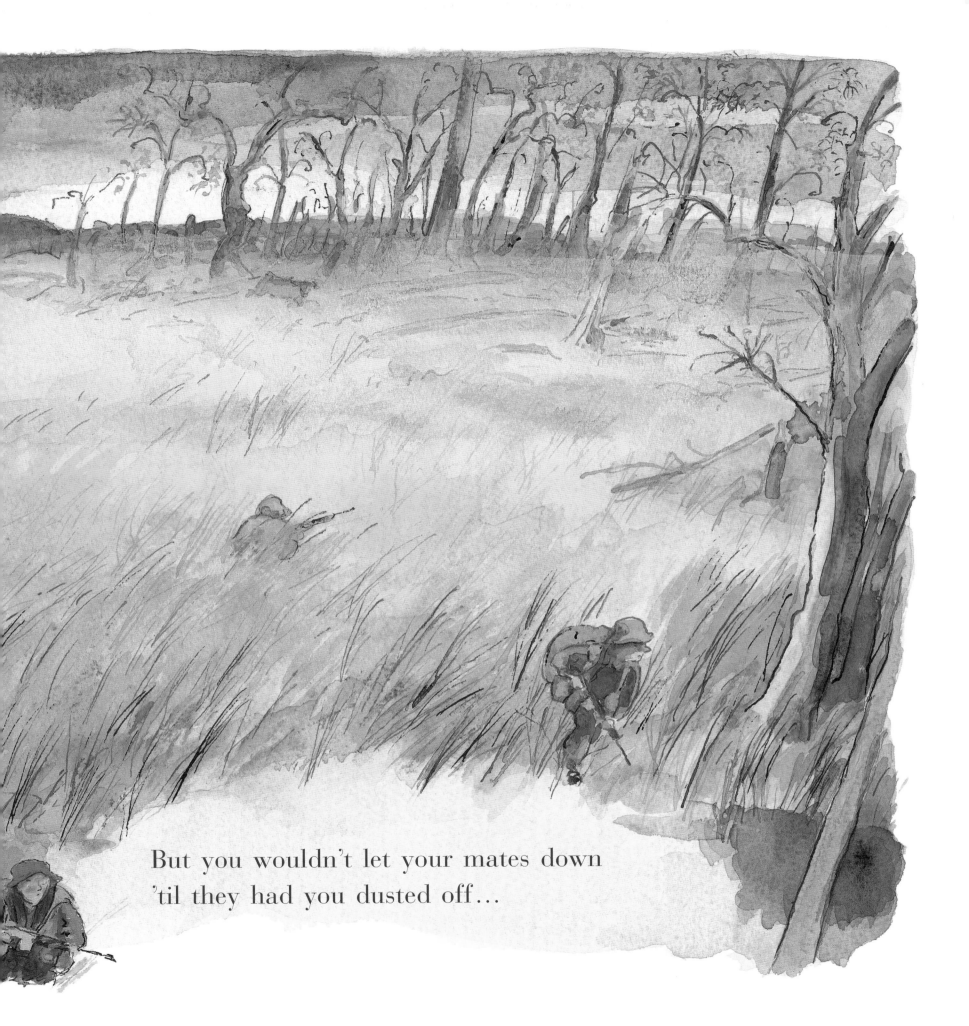

But you wouldn't let your mates down
'til they had you dusted off...

...so you closed your eyes and thought about something else.

Then someone yelled out 'Contact', and the bloke behind me swore.

We hooked in there for hours...

...then a God almighty roar.

Frankie kicked a mine the day that mankind kicked the moon.

God help me, he was going home in June.

I can still see Frankie,
drinking tinnies in the Grand Hotel
on a thirty-six hour rec leave in Vung Tau.

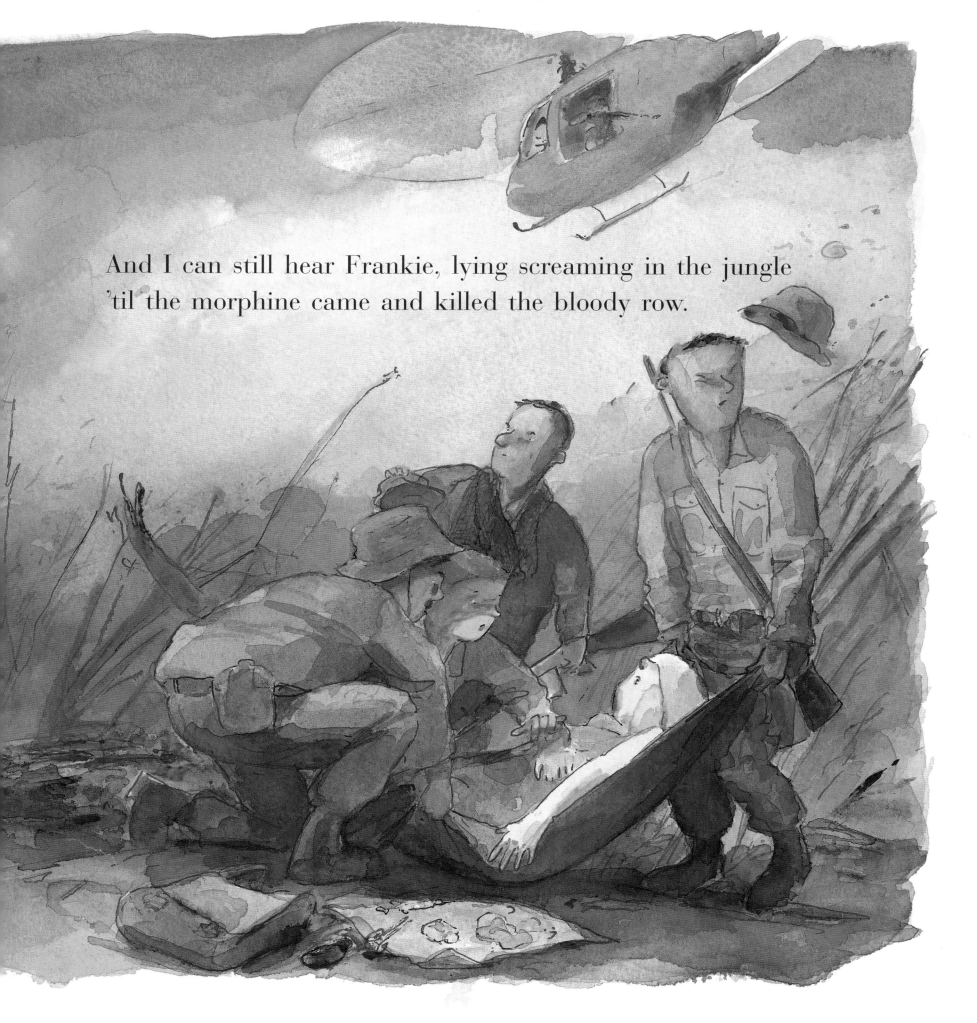

And I can still hear Frankie, lying screaming in the jungle
'til the morphine came and killed the bloody row.

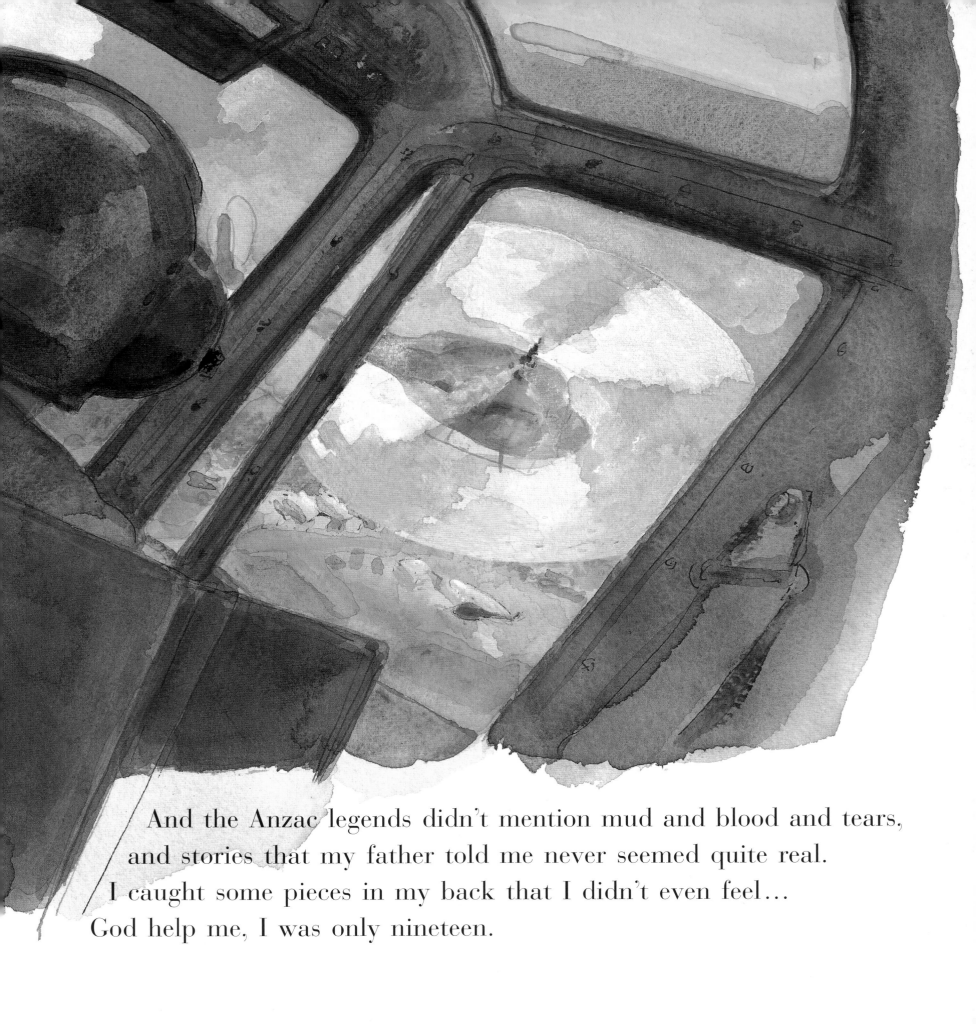

And the Anzac legends didn't mention mud and blood and tears,
and stories that my father told me never seemed quite real.
I caught some pieces in my back that I didn't even feel...
God help me, I was only nineteen.

And can you tell me, doctor, why I still can't get to sleep?
And why the Channel Seven chopper chills me to my feet?
And what's this rash that comes and goes – can you tell me what it means?

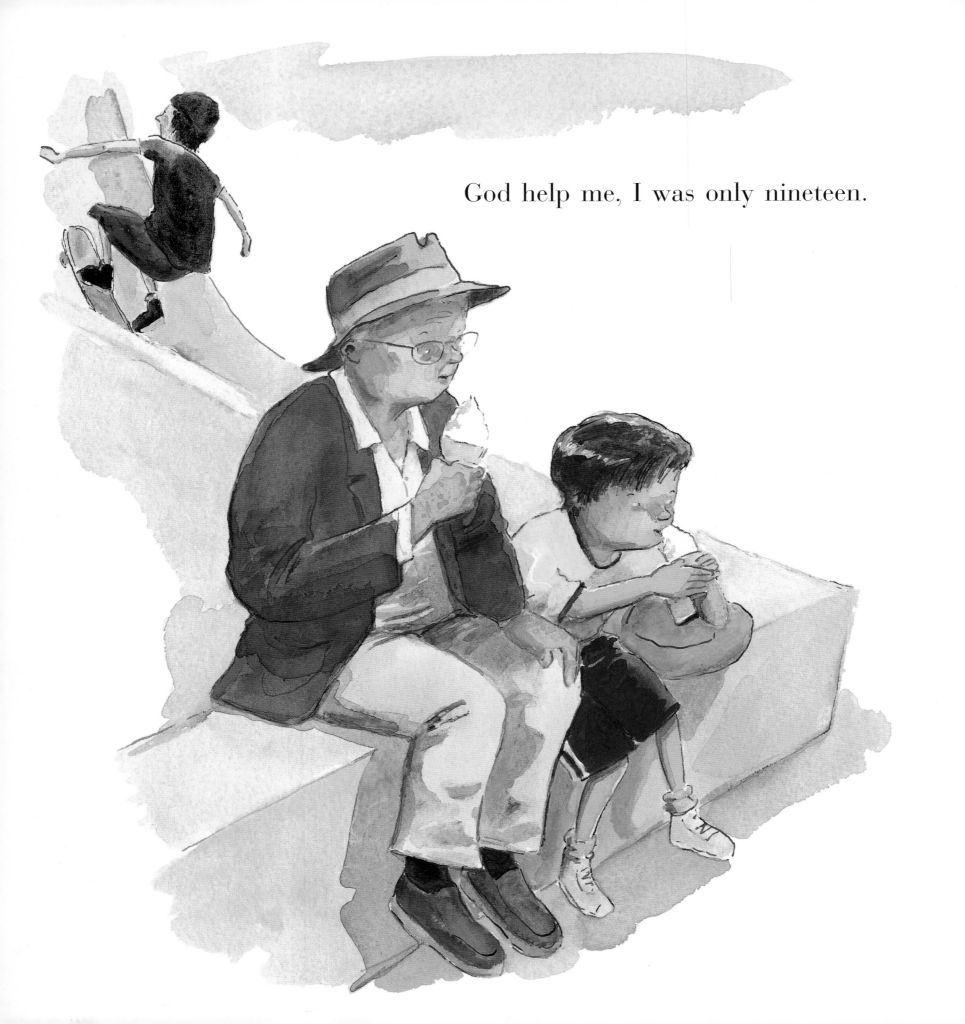

God help me, I was only nineteen.

G'day,

In 1968, I was in high school and the Vietnam War was in full swing. Lots of young Australian men were being shipped off to Asia. My mum was really frightened that, in a few years, I would have to join them.

Not everyone agreed that Australia should be fighting in this war. Pretty soon, thousands of people were marching through Australian cities and towns to demonstrate against it.

By January 1973, Australia had pulled all its forces out of Vietnam. But our servicemen and women weren't welcomed home like Australians had been from earlier wars, and I remember feeling very sorry for them. They'd come back sick and injured from an unpopular war and it seemed like the rest of us didn't want to know.

In 1981, I met Denny, my future wife. Her brother, Mick, had fought in Vietnam, and in 1969 he'd been involved in a very serious land-mine incident in the Long Hai Hills.

After Mick and I got to be mates, I told him I'd always wanted to write a song about the Australians who fought in Vietnam. I asked him if he would tell me his story. He agreed, and one night we recorded a long, long conversation about his year there. I reckon I listened to that recording a hundred times or more.

Sometimes songs take months to write. Sometimes they just tumble out. When I actually sat down to write 'I Was Only 19', it took me fifteen minutes. It was that quick.

'I Was Only 19' has received a lot of praise from veterans. Perhaps this is because the song reminds us that we can oppose a war vigorously but we must always support the people we send to fight it.

In lots of ways, '19' changed my life. Because of this song, I've met some wonderful people, I've been to some amazing places and I've done some amazing things. But the greatest pleasure I get is when I'm recognised out of the blue by veterans and their families and thanked so warmly and genuinely. I have a lot of veteran mates now, and they are always there for me when it feels like the wind's blowing in the wrong direction.

Thirty years later, it's important to remember the courage and trust Mick showed when he stepped outside the closed circle of Vietnam veterans to tell me his story. We all owe him.

Oh, and one last thing — don't let anyone ever tell you that songs can't change the world.